ELEPHANT & MOUSE

GET READY FOR
EASTER

by
Lois G. Grambling
Illustrated by Deborah Maze

BARRON'S

New York • London • Toronto • Sydney

All inquiries should be addressed to:
Barron's Educational Series, Inc.
250 Wireless Boulevard
Hauppauge, NY 11788

International Standard Book No. 0-8120-9186-8

International Standard Book No. 0-8120-6200-0

Library of Congress Catalog Card No. 90-48949

Library of Congress Cataloging-in-Publication Data

Grambling, Lois G.
     Elephant and Mouse get ready for Easter / by Lois G. Grambling;
illustrated by Deborah Maze.
          p.   cm.
          Summary: Elephant and Mouse borrow colored eggs from a robin, a
cardinal and a bobolink so that they can make a thank-you basket for
Easter Rabbit that will surprise him when he returns from his Easter
deliveries.
     ISBN 0-8120-6200-0
     [1. Gratitude—Fiction.   2. Easter eggs—Fiction.]   I. Maze,
Deborah, ill.   II. Title.
PZ7.G7655Eo   1991
[E]—dc20   90-48949
                                                                      CIP
PRINTED IN HONG KONG   AC

1234 4900 987654321

For my favorite little Easter bunnies
Lara and Tyler

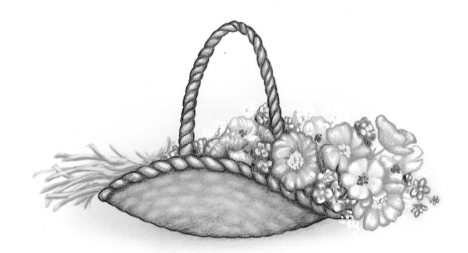

"Tomorrow is Easter," said Elephant.
"So it is," said Mouse.
"Easter Rabbit will be bringing us colored eggs for our baskets," said Elephant.
"He always remembers," said Mouse.
"He never forgets," said Elephant.

"Wouldn't it be nice if we left a basket of colored eggs for
Easter Rabbit on his doorstep tomorrow?" asked Elephant.
"That would be very nice," said Mouse. "But where
would we get the eggs?"
"Why from Hen, of course!" said Elephant.

Elephant and Mouse hurried over to Hen's house.
They knocked on Hen's door.
Hen answered.

"Good afternoon, Hen," said Elephant and Mouse.
"Good afternoon, Elephant and Mouse," said Hen.
"Do you have some eggs we could color for
Easter Rabbit's basket?" asked Elephant.
"We want to surprise Easter Rabbit with
his own basket tomorrow," said Mouse.

"That would be a lovely
surprise," said Hen.
"I would give you some
eggs if I could," she said.
"But I can't. I have no eggs lef
I gave them all to Easter Rabb
yesterday."

"Thank you anyway," said Elephant
and Mouse politely.
And they left Hen's house sadly.

"How can we surprise Easter Rabbit
with a basket of colored eggs tomorrow
if we have no eggs to color?" asked
Elephant.
"We can't," answered Mouse.

Suddenly Elephant smiled.
"I have an idea, Mouse," he said.
"Splendid," said Mouse. "You almost
always do!"
And Elephant told Mouse his idea.
Then Mouse smiled, too.

Elephant and Mouse hurried back to their house.
They hurried out to their yard and over to the
apple tree where Robin had built her nest.
Robin was sitting in her nest when they got there.

"Good afternoon, Robin," said
Elephant and Mouse.
"Good afternoon, Elephant and Mouse,"
said Robin.
"Would you let us have one of your
colored eggs for Easter Rabbit's basket?"
asked Elephant.
"We want to surprise Easter Rabbit with
his own basket tomorrow," said Mouse.

"That would be a lovely surprise,"
said Robin.
"That COULD be a very lovely surprise!"
she said smiling.
"I will give you one of my eggs. But you
must promise to take good care of it."
"Oh, we will," said Elephant.
"We certainly will," said Mouse.
And Robin gave Elephant and Mouse
one of her eggs.

Elephant and Mouse carefully put Robin's pale blue egg in Easter Rabbit's basket. Easter Rabbit's basket now had one colored egg in it.

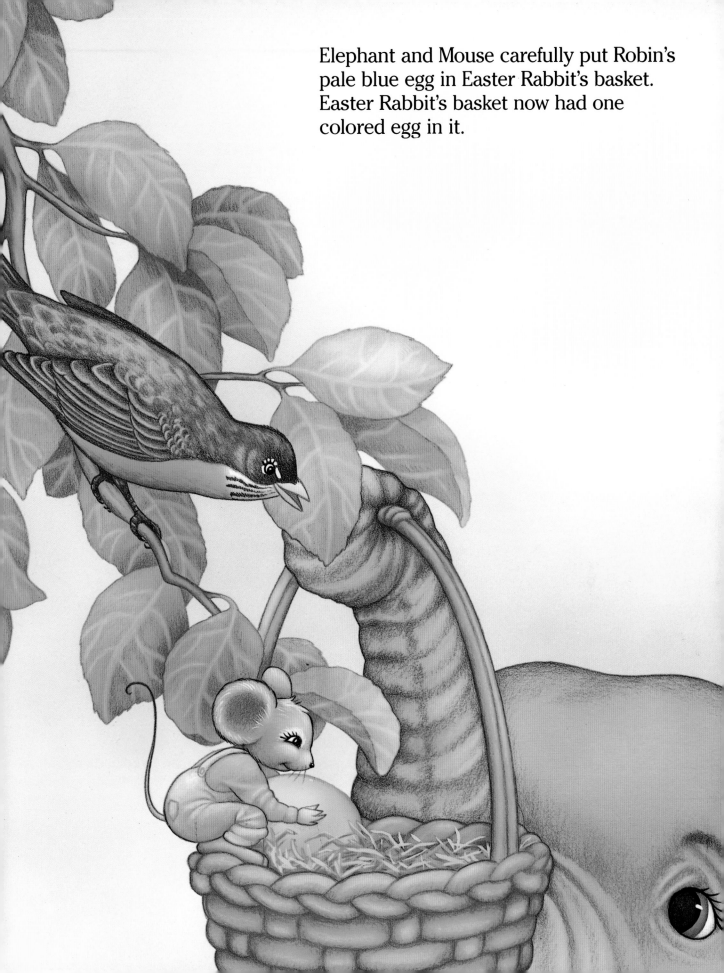

Next, Elephant and Mouse hurried over to the
brushy thicket where Cardinal had built her nest.
Cardinal was sitting in her nest when they got there.

"Good afternoon, Cardinal," said
Elephant and Mouse.
"Good afternoon, Elephant and
Mouse," said Cardinal.
"Would you let us have one of your
colored eggs for Easter Rabbit's basket?"
asked Elephant.
"We want to surprise Easter Rabbit with his
own basket tomorrow," said Mouse.

"That would be a lovely surprise," said Cardinal.
"That COULD be a very lovely surprise!" she said smiling.

"I will give you one of my eggs.
But you must promise to take
good care of it."
"Oh, we will," said Elephant.
"We certainly will," said Mouse.
And Cardinal gave Elephant and
Mouse one of her eggs.
Elephant and Mouse carefully put
Cardinal's spotted green egg
in Easter Rabbit's basket.
Easter Rabbit's basket now
had two colored eggs in it.

Next, Elephant and Mouse hurried over to the meadow where Bobolink had built her nest.
Bobolink was sitting in her nest when they got there.

"Good afternoon, Bobolink," said Elephant and Mouse.
"Good afternoon, Elephant and Mouse," said Bobolink.
"Would you let us have one of your colored eggs for
Easter Rabbit's basket?" asked Elephant.
"We want to surprise Easter Rabbit with his
own basket tomorrow," said Mouse.

"That would be a lovely surprise,"
said Bobolink.
"That COULD be a very lovely surprise!"
she said smiling.
"I will give you one of my eggs. But you must
promise to take good care of it."
"Oh, we will," said Elephant.
"We certainly will," said Mouse.
And Bobolink gave Elephant and Mouse
one of her eggs.

Elephant and Mouse carefully put
Bobolink's blue and purple egg in
Easter Rabbit's basket.
Easter Rabbit's basket now had three
colored eggs in it.

"That should do it," said Elephant,
looking at the eggs in the basket.
"That should do it nicely," said Mouse,
looking at the eggs in the basket.

The next morning Elephant and Mouse
got up early.
They hurried over to Easter Rabbit's house.
They wanted to get there before Easter
Rabbit returned from his morning deliveries.

Elephant looked around.
"Good," he said. "Easter Rabbit is
still out. He'll certainly be surprised
when he sees this."
"He certainly will!" agreed Mouse.
And Elephant and Mouse put the
basket with the colored eggs in it on
Easter Rabbit's doorstep.

"We'd better hide now before he returns,"
said Elephant.
"We'd better," said Mouse.
Elephant hid behind a big tree.
Mouse hid behind a little tree.

A few minutes later Easter Rabbit came hopping down
the path to his house.

"What's this?" he asked, seeing the basket
on his doorstep.
He read the note attached to the
basket's handle.

DEAR EASTER RABBIT,
THIS IS FOR YOU.
IT IS FROM YOUR FRIENDS.
HAPPY EASTER!

Easter Rabbit looked around.
He didn't see anyone.
He looked around again.
He still didn't see anyone.

But he smiled anyway and said,
"Thank you, Friends . . .
Thank you . . . wherever you are.
These are lovely eggs.
The loveliest eggs I have ever seen!"

Dear
Easter Rabbit,
This is for you.
It is from
your friends.
HAPPY EASTER!

And just as Easter Rabbit
said this,
the three eggs in his basket
began to crack open . . .
one by one.

Crack!
CRACK! !
CRACK! ! !

And three tiny birds
appeared!

The three tiny birds began
to sing joyfully.
And suddenly Easter
morning was filled with the
happy sound of their music!

ster Rabbit was delighted.
is face glowed with pleasure.

"These are indeed lovely eggs,"
he said.
"The loveliest eggs I have ever
HEARD!
Thank you again, Friends.
Thank you wherever you are.
I'll never forget this musical Easter.
Never, ever!"

"Nor shall we," said Elephant and Mouse, coming out from behind the big tree and the little tree where they had been hiding. "Never, ever!"

Robin and Cardinal and Bobolink flew
down from the nearby tree branch
where they had been watching.
"That is how we hoped it would be,"
they said, smiling.
"HAPPY EASTER!"

"HAPPY EASTER!" said
Elephant and Mouse.
"HAPPY EASTER!"
said Easter Rabbit.

The three tiny birds started to sing again.
And . . .
Elephant and Mouse
and Easter Rabbit
and Robin and Cardinal and Bobolink
gathered around the basket
to listen.